ANGIE MORGAN trained in Graphic Design and
Illustration at Goldsmith's College. Her inspiration comes
from her three grown-up children and from the children at
her local primary school, where she offers Maths and
Literacy support. This is Angie Morgan's second picture book for
Frances Lincoln, following *Daisy's Big Dig*. She lives in Bath.

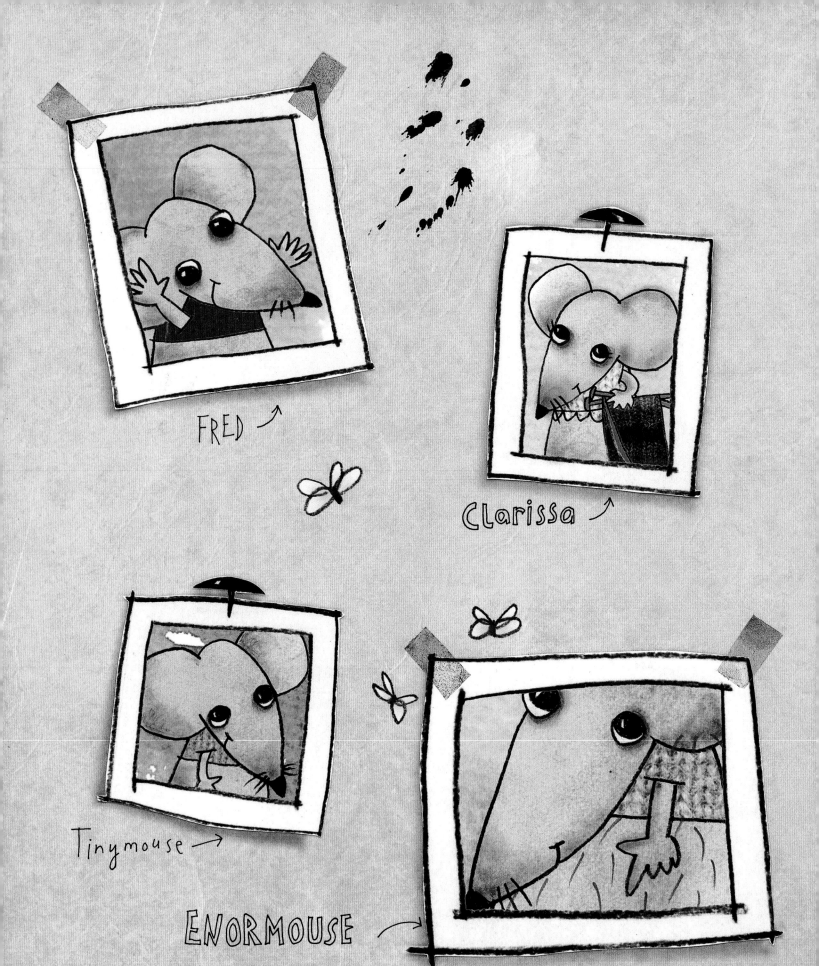

FRED ↗

Clarissa ↗

Tinymouse →

ENORMOUSE ↷

For Joel
(who gave me the idea)

and Hannah
(because it was her rat)

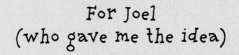

JANETTA OTTER-BARRY BOOKS

Text and illustrations copyright © Angie Morgan 2013
The right of Angie Morgan to be identified as the author
and illustrator of this Work has been asserted by her
in accordance with the Copyright, Designs
and Patents Act, 1988 (United Kingdom).

First published in Great Britain in 2013 and in the USA in 2014 by
Frances Lincoln Children's Books,
74-77 White Lion Street, London N1 9PF
www.franceslincoln.com

First published in paperback in Great Britain and in the USA in 2014.

A CIP catalogue record for this book is available from the British Library.

ISBN 978-1-84780-526-3

Printed in China

1 3 5 7 9 8 6 4 2

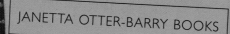

ENOR**M**OUSE

ANGIE MORGAN

F

FRANCES LINCOLN
CHILDREN'S BOOKS

Enormouse was
BIG.
He didn't know why.
He just was.

His best friend Tinymouse
tried to help.

"Don't worry, Enormouse.
Being big isn't SO bad."

And it wasn't.
Being big was
really quite useful.

When he went exploring
with the other mice
he could reach things
they couldn't reach.

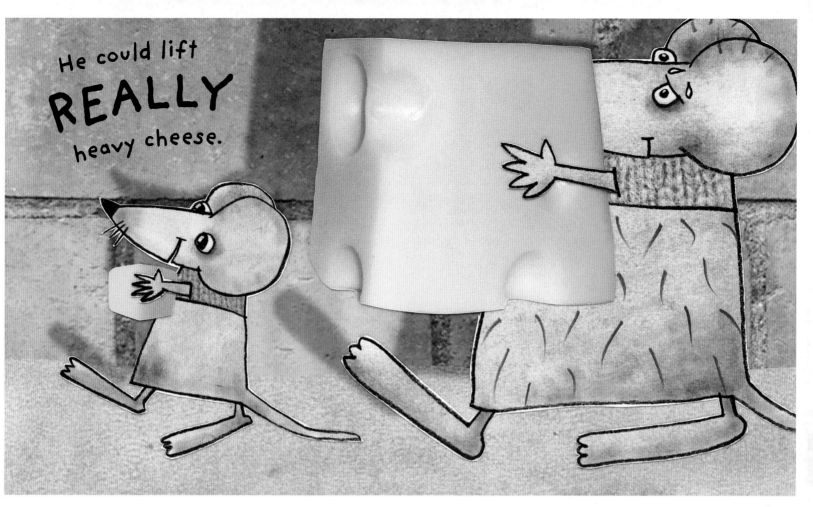

He could lift **REALLY** heavy cheese.

He could carry the little mice when their legs got tired.

RATS
The Common Rat
(Rattus Norvegicus)

One day, when Enormouse
was exploring with Tinymouse,
they came across a large book.

The two friends looked at
the pictures. They looked
at each other.

Rats are bigger th
long snouts, co
scaly tails. They lik
or rubbish dum
find their fo
anything
food that
covered

"I think I know why you're so big, Enormouse. You're not a mouse at all... You're a **RAT!**"

MICE
The House Mouse
(Mus musculus)

Mice are smaller than **rats**. They have pointy snouts and shiny **black eyes** like beads. They have **large ears** and soft **fur**. They **steal** their food

...from **humans** and especially like **chocolate** and **apples**. They make their **homes** under **floors** or in garden **sheds** and they keep them very **clean** and **tidy**.

...ce. They have ...c fur and ...ive near **dustbins** ...nich is where they They will eat they **specially like** ...ouldy and **smelly** and ...ies. ...nerally friendly but have ...ers and **never** say please

When the other mice
found out they laughed.

Poor Enormouse.

All his life he had
thought he was a mouse.

Being a rat was rather a shock.

"I don't think I belong in the Mouse House any more," he said to himself sadly.

"I think I should go and find some rats to live with."

So Enormouse left the Mouse House.

At first he felt afraid and rather lonely.

But a friendly rat came by who kindly took him to the Rats' House.

When they arrived
Enormouse was horrified.
There was mess EVERYWHERE!

It wasn't messy like an untidy bedroom.
It was MUCH worse.
It was a MOULDY, SMELLY,
BUZZING with FLIES sort of mess.

The smell was so bad it made
Enormouse's eyes water.

He thought he ought to ask
if they would like him to
do a spot of cleaning.
But the rats only laughed.

Poor Enormouse. He just wasn't like the other rats. His heart ached for Tinymouse, his other mouse friends and his cosy home.

He began to think he had been a bit hasty.

Back at the Mouse House the mice were all VERY sorry that they had laughed at Enormouse.

So they all
set off bravely.

None of them had the
faintest idea where
they were going...

...and soon they were all
very, very lost.

In the Rats' House, Enormouse finally knew what he had to do.

He said goodbye to the rats, thanked them politely for having him, and set off home.

"GOODBYE!"

Meanwhile, in the dark,
the mice were very frightened.

They began to hear strange
and scary noises all around.

An owl hooted in a tree.

"HELP!" they squeaked.
"We're all going to die!"

Suddenly they heard footsteps
approaching and a LARGE
shadow LOOMED over them.

There was much trembling
and squeaking and a small
voice said...

"I wish Enormouse was here.
He would save us."

So Enormouse did.
He was back where
he truly belonged.

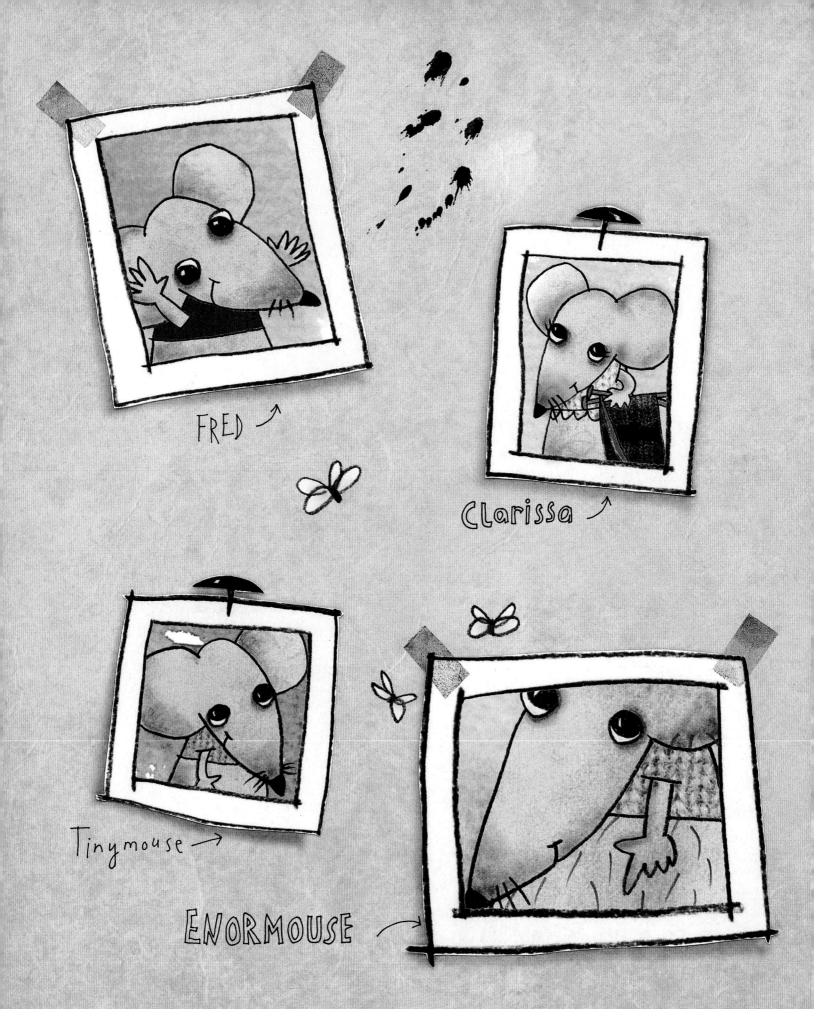

FRED →

Clarissa →

Tinymouse →

ENORMOUSE →

MORE PICTURE BOOKS FROM FRANCES LINCOLN CHILDREN'S BOOKS

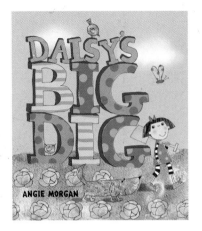

978-1-84780-463-1

Daisy's Big Dig
Angie Morgan

The people who live in Daisy's street never ever talk to each other. But Daisy has a big plan to bring everyone together – a Digging Party! Will you come too?

"What a wonderful treat for KS1 pupils! A modern fairy tale, a book full of community spirit that will melt the heart of every cynic."
— *The School Librarian*

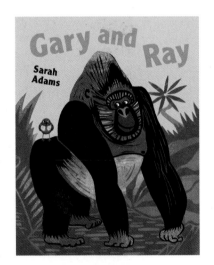

978-1-84780-260-6

Gary and Ray
Sarah Adams

Gary the gorilla is the only animal in the jungle who doesn't have a friend. Even the children of the village are afraid of him. He wishes everyone could see that he is lonely and afraid too. Then one day a tiny sunbird flies down to say hello and an unusual friendship grows.

"This sweet story will resonate with many."
— *Booklist*

Frances Lincoln titles are available from all good bookshops.
You can also buy books and find out more about your favourite titles,
authors and illustrators on our website: www.franceslincoln.com